HIGH PRAISE FOR THE ORIGINAL MUSICAL STAGE PLAY FROM THE 2023 AUSTIN FILM FESTIVAL SCRIPT COMPETITION

"In a homage to the beloved show "I Love Lucy," a witty woman in her forties ponders the purpose of her life and unexpectedly falls for a charming performer. The story is captivating, with skillful dialogue that brings the characters' world to life. This screenplay is truly compelling."

"This script is an original homage that displays a unique and fresh voice. It is a romantic comedy and a story of female empowerment. The writer incorporates laughs, witty banter, and delivers a funny message about the nature of love and a successful life."

"The standout element of this screenplay is its dialogue. The writer's voice shines through, with witty conversations that explore the theme of societal expectations of true love. The world-building is fantastic, evoking the atmosphere of a 1920s art deco bar with Flapper women embracing their sexual strength."

"The dialogue in this piece is fantastic, with a natural and energetic delivery. The writer has a gift for crafting snappy conversations and the back-and-forth flow of natural banter. The characters are witty, and their discussions are filled with wit."

"Ellen and Grant are compelling protagonists with a witty relationship that is perfect for a rom-com. Their dynamic is exciting, fresh, and their playful banter makes them easy to invest in. Their shared goal of making a show together and falling in love is more than enough to carry a feature film."

Just For Love,
A Moment In Time

Original Musical Stage Play

by

Librettist and Composer
Len Guardino

Just For Love, A Moment In Time
Original Musical Stage Play,
written by Len Guardino.

Cover photography by Alessandro Biascioli, licensed
by DepositPhotos.

MANUFACTURED AND PRINTED
IN THE UNITED STATES OF AMERICA

First Edition, 2025

ISBN 13: 979-8-218-89866-3 (Paperback edition)
ISBN 13: 979-8-218-90203-2 (eBook edition)
ISBN 13: 979-8-279-60602-3 (Barnes & Noble
Paperback edition)
Library of Congress Control No.: 2025927813
UPC: CC-B-4-JFLAMIT-OSP-EB

A Note About The Music

All of the words and music in the original play and referenced in this work were composed by playwright/librettist and composer, Len Guardino. The words and music are available for purchase from the author's/publisher's website at https://champagnecat.com/words-and-music-by-len-guardino/ and sold either separately or as a set with the paperback book, and include the following works:

1.   "Just For Love," © by Len Guardino;
2.   "I Want Someone To Love Me," © by Len Guardino;
3.   "Loving You," © by Len Guardino;
4.   "You're Mine," © by Len Guardino;
5.   "I Want It All," © by Len Guardino;
6.   "When A Love Like Ours Begins," © by Len Guardino;
7.   "A Moment In Time," © by Len Guardino; and
8.   "She Never Really Tried," © by Len Guardino.

Please contact the publisher for licensing at admin@champagnecat.com.

Just For Love,
A Moment In Time

*Our Tomorrows Are Today
and Tomorrow*

MANHATTAN HOTEL - NIGHT

We are in the lobby of this deluxe midtown hotel.
Well-appointed patrons of the hotel come and go, the
front desk is very busy. It is obviously a popular,
sophisticated establishment.

We TRACK through the hotel, arriving at the Grand
Ball Room. The doors swing outward and two women
appear: ELLEN TAYLOR and MARY KOHLER. Ellen is
blonde and pretty, with a warm smile while Mary is a
tall, striking brunette. They are both in their late
thirties, dressed in flamboyant costumes – garish
dresses, big hats, lots of makeup – and come sailing
out of the ballroom doors; they have just come from
the annual charity ball of their women's club. Ellen
glances over at Mary.

ELLEN

What's the matter, Mary?

MARY

Ellen, we wasted another day of our lives.

ELLEN

You sound like a soap opera. That wasn't a waste of
time. Think of all the money our club raised, Mary.
Tonight's affair was for a good

2

cause.

MARY

I wouldn't exactly call it an affair.

ELLEN

Really? It looked like you were having an affair to me.
The way you were dancing with that little man . . .
cheek to breast.

She laughs.

MARY

Oh, you mean my breast friend? Did you see him? He
never even bent his legs when he danced. That wasn't
the only thing that was stiff. Did you see his stiff . . .
upper lip?

She laughs.

ELLEN

Mary, that's called 'the old money look.'

MARY

Old money, new money! This is the last time I give
my time and body to charity. I'm just not coming
anymore.

ELLEN

Mary, bite your tongue.

MARY

Ellen, I can't afford to waste time. I'm 39 years old.
39. Do you know what that means?

ELLEN

It means that next year you'll have to have your eyes
done again.

MARY

It means I'm going to be . . . 40 years old.

ELLEN

Mary, your life is just beginning. 40 years old?

MARY

Does this look like a body that's just beginning? I have
more lines on my face than the front page of The
New York Times. (She points to her forehead.) Look at
these lines.

ELLEN

Good god! Look at those head lines! Mary

4

Kohler, a wasted life if ever there was one. All the poor girl has is a good husband, great kids, a huge, beautiful house

(Ellen looks at Mary's hand).

A gorgeous diamond ring. A good, small, perfect, recycled nose. A good pair of silicon implants?

(she shakes her head in disbelief). Mary, do you remember how miserable you used to be? Before you were married?

MARY

Ellen, I'm serious.

ELLEN

Maybe all you need is a good -

MARY

When did you last have a good one?

ELLEN

Let me think. Monday night . . . 8:30 P.M. . . . five years ago. I think it was a good one.

MARY

How can you tell?

ELLEN

He had a-smile on his face.

MARY

I'm beginning to think they don't exist.

ELLEN

They <u>must</u> exist! I can't believe all that huffing and puffing is done just to blow our stomachs up. Mary, maybe all you have is indigestion. Too much rich French food. It's your grandmother's fault. If she had come over on the Mayflower and from Paris instead of Poland.

MARY

Ellen, what have we accomplished?

ELLEN

What do you mean, what have we accomplished? We figured out that your problem is not in your head, but in your stomach. All you need is a little Maalox.

6

ELLEN (CONT'D)

If the fire spreads a little lower, then we're in trouble.

MARY

Ellen, what have we accomplished in life?

ELLEN

Mary, what do you want? You want to be queen of Long Island? You want to be an astronaut? What? A lion tamer? For your birthday I'll buy you a lion, how's that?

MARY

My life is dull, empty, meaningless.

ELLEN

So I'll buy you two lions. And some whips and chains.

MARY

I'm afraid I'm going to look in the mirror one day and my reflection is going to say: "Mary, what would you do if you had your life to live over again?" And while I'm thinking of an answer, my reflection starts laughing. "Sorry

Mary, you fool, you wasted too much time. It's too late."

ELLEN

You just tell that mirror that Mary Kohler isn't wasting her life. She's a great mother, a great wife, a great friend, and one day you'll have <u>great</u> grandchildren.

MARY

That's what they told my Russian grandmother.

ELLEN

And let's not forget Mary the dancer.

She mimics Mary dancing with the short man.

MARY

That's right, I am a good dancer. I could have been a professional dancer, that's how good I am. Tonight, watching everyone dancing in their costumes I remembered how I loved to dance when I was a kid. I should be touring Europe - with a ballet company.

ELLEN

Touring Europe with a ballet company? Mary, get
real! Do you know how many professional dancers
would love to trade places with us? I bet right now
there are thousands, millions of professional dancers
all over Long Island who are saying, "Boy, do I wish I
could be Mary Kohler. I wish I had a fantastic family.
I wish I had a fantastic home. I wish I had a husband
who loved me."

MARY

Do you know what?

(Ellen gives her a look like "I don't want to know.")

I don't love my husband. I don't like my home. I hate
my kids.

ELLEN

Hate is a pretty strong word, Mary.

MARY

Okay, let's put it this way -- they Annoy me. How's
that?

ELLEN

Well, none out of three, that's bad.

MARY

Funny thing is, he probably feels the same way. We're both afraid to admit it.

ELLEN

Maybe all you need is a vacation. Go off on your own, get it out of your system.

MARY

Ellen, I don't think you understand. I don't want to be alone.

ELLEN

So take the kids with you!

MARY

I'm not happy. I want to be in love.

Mary starts to sing and dance to "I Want Someone To Love Me." When she's done, Ellen applauds.

10

MARY

(continuing, on a roll)

I want to do things with my mind and body. Things
I've only dreamed about.

ELLEN

What!

(she starts laughing)

Mary, you want to do something with your body?
Donate it to science?

MARY

(sighing)

I might as well, for all the use it gets.

ELLEN <u>You are a soap opera!</u>

MARY

Ellen, do you know that my husband has never seen
me completely naked? On our honeymoon I didn't
want my husband to know I wore a girdle so I
wrapped it in towels and hid it under the bed. The
cleaning people took

MARY (CONT'D)

it down to the laundry room. It took me three hours to sort through the laundry. God forbid I should let him see that I wore that rubber amour. That was my shield of protection. I never thought that my you know what was something to be proud of. I thought it was to be guarded and hidden, like some deep, dark secret.

ELLEN

Mary, what kind of a deep, dark secret? Four kids came out of there. Your diamond ring. Your mink coat. Your new car, your...

MARY

Stop it, you're making me nervous.

ELLEN

Feel this!

(Mary touches her waist.)

MARY

What is it?

12

ELLEN

What is it? It's my girdle! You think you're the only
one who's perfect? And as for my husband seeing me
completely naked, I haven't seen myself completely
naked. Mary, no one is completely anything. Healthy,
wealthy, happy

MARY

What about <u>you?</u>

ELLEN

You want to trade places? I'm happy. Not ecstatic, but
happy. I'm not a dreamer or a poet...

(she turns to the hotel bell hop) Excuse me, where's
the Ladies Room?

The bellhop points straight ahead.

MARY

Ellen, do you remember what that psychic said? She
said I would meet my soul mate and he would change
my life. (Mary looks in her bag and pulls out a piece
of paper.) Look. Brown hair, green eyes, intelligent,
attractive.

ELLEN

Mary, she told me the same thing.

(Ellen pulls a corresponding piece of paper out of her
bag.)

The same thing, only my soul mate apparently will
be wearing a flower. Probably in his hair. Mary, she
tells everyone the same thing. It's a female fantasy. I
can't believe that someone as intelligent as you would
believe what some psychic tells her.

(Ellen pretends she is the psychic by peering at
Mary's palm.)

Mary Kohler, I see a man. Yes, there he is. He's
reading a book. No, it's Playboy magazine. So he must
be intelligent. Let's see. He has green eyes. No, one
eye is green, the other one is bloodshot. Too much
centerfold. And he has a stiff . . . upper lip.

(she laughs)

14

He's trying to tell you something.

(Ellen puts her ear to Mary's hand.) Yes, what is it,
soul mate? Schmuck, schmuck! (Ellen drops Mary's
hand, they're both laughing.) Mary, for a moment
there you had me worried. I thought you were
serious. Psychics. Soul mates. Ballet companies.
Poems. We could have a garage sale with your
fantasies.

MARY

Ellen, you think it's funny but what would you do if
you met your soul mate?

ELLEN

I already have and he answers to 'my husband.'

MARY

He doesn't have brown hair. As a matter of fact, he
doesn't have any hair!

ELLEN

Where is it written that soul mates must have hair?
What do you want anyway, a soul mate or a primate?

MARY

Ellen, I'm serious. What would you do if you met someone who swept you off your feet?

ELLEN

If he can rake leaves as well as sweep I guess I'd reconsider.

MARY

Well, if I met my soul mate, I would -

ELLEN

Would what? Leave your husband? Abandon your children? Let another woman move into your home? Mary, bite your tongue. All for what? Passion. (They look at each other and smile.) Strike passion. For what? A soul mate? Now I know you're kidding. Mary, you're dreaming. We're adults. Responsible parents, wives. You know life. Love is not passion. You sound like you're in heat. Mary, you're a human being. You know love is in the universe. The continuum of the human spirit. The eternal flow of all living matter . . .

MARY

What!?

16

ELLEN

Relax, we're having a great time. we have fantastic lives. Stop fantasizing.

MARY

Ellen, you think you have all the answers don't you?

ELLEN

No, I just think I can control my emotions better than you can. Mary, what I'm trying to say is that there's more to life than storybook love. Knights in shining armor. Soul mates. Sex.

MARY (laughing)

There is?

ELLEN

Sure there is. There's . . . ah, ahh . . .

(They both laugh.)

INT. LADIES ROOM, HOTEL - NIGHT

They have arrived at the Ladies Room. One door leads
into the Ladies Room, the other door leads to the
hotel's nightclub.

MARY

(Eyeing the nightclub door) Come on, super lady. I'll
buy you a drink.

ELLEN

(Looking at her watch)

It's getting late. It's almost 9:30. Let's go to the Ladies
Room and then go home.

Ellen pulls Mary toward the Ladies Room. Mary pulls
Ellen into the nightclub.

MARY

Come on, let's celebrate our . . . my liberation from
childhood dreams. We're adults.

They both laugh and go into the club where everyone
stares at them in their costumes.

ELLEN

Let's get out of here.

18

MARY

One drink. And then we'll go back to the good life.

A burly drunk with a full head of hair and wearing a flower in his lapel starts to tease Ellen and Mary.

BURLY DRUNK

Well, if it isn't Cinderella and her fairy godmother.

ELLEN

(pointing to burly drunk)

Mary, look at that head of hair! Maybe he's your soul mate.

MARY

But he's wearing a flower, maybe he's yours.

They both crack up.

BARTENDER

What would you ladies like to drink?

MARY

Scotch and water for me please. Ellen, what are you having?

ELLEN

Mary, let's go, it's getting late.

MARY

What do you want to drink?

ELLEN

You know I don't drink.

MARY

Come on, we agreed. One drink and then we leave.

ELLEN

Okay, what comes in the smallest glass?

BURLY DRUNK

(to the bartender) Give her a pina colada.

20

A MALE

(offering Ellen his seat) Would you like to sit down?

ELLEN

No thank you, we're married, I mean, we're leaving in a moment.

MARY

Ellen, talk to him! He's cute! He looks like he can rake leaves.

(Ellen switches places with Mary.)

MARY (to the male)

Can you rake leaves?

MALE

(to Mary)

What's the matter with your friend?

MARY

Nothing. She's just a little shy when it comes to men with hair.

(Ellen is looking at her watch again.)

MARY

Ellen, relax, you're making me nervous again.

ELLEN

Mary, let's go to the Ladies Room. (The Burly Drunk overhears this.)

BURLY DRUNK

I'll show you to the Ladies Room.

MARY

Thank you but I can go by myself.

BURLY DRUNK

I said I would show you, not go with you!

The people seated at the bar laugh.

ELLEN

I'm sure I can find it myself.

(Ellen rises and makes her way from the bar. Her eyes haven't adjusted to the dimmed lights and she bypasses the door to the Ladies Room and walks straight ahead into the main room of the cabaret where we hear, and then see, a male, center-stage, singing "Just For Love," to an attractive woman in the audience.)

INT. CABARET ROOM - NIGHT

The room is dark and quiet. Ellen crosses through the center of the tabled area. She stops, blocking the spotlight away from the singer. The audience is laughing at her. She's blinded by the spotlight and starts bumping into tables and trips backward into the singer. He stops singing and tries to catch her. They both fall. Her hoop skirt is up in the air. The audience is laughing. She stands up with the help of the club manager ànd one of the waiters. Her face is covered by her hat. She's dizzy and holds on to a chair, rubbing the top of her head.

ELLEN

(looking in the singer's direction) Where am I?

GRANT

(the singer)

You're in the middle of my act.

ELLEN

Did I miss much?

GRANT

No, not too much. Maybe one table.

ELLEN

Very funny, a singing clown!

GRANT

Who taught you how to walk? King Kong?

ELLEN

Who taught you how to sing? A rooster?

(The audience loves their exchange. Ellen tries to straighten her hat so she can see. She sways to one side. The manager and Grant try to grab her. Grant grabs her sleeve. We hear it rip. She hears the rip but doesn't know where it is. She touches her vital areas, trying to find the rip in her dress. The audience is now roaring with laughter.

GRANT

(to Ellen)

Let me help you.

(She still can't see him, he's teasing her, playing the audience. He touches her stomach.)

ELLEN

Leave me alone, you pervert!

(She swings her wand, she still can't see. Grant ducks. She hits the manager. She thinks he's Grant. The manager has a flower in his lapel and he wears a toupee. He's trying to put it back in place. It's sitting crooked on his head.)

ELLEN

(To the manager . . .)

Now you can finish your act, you creep!

(She pulls his toupee down over his eyes. The audience loves it.)

MANAGER

(Speaking in a gravelly voice.) She's crazy!

ELLEN

What happened to your voice?

Grant is behind her.

GRANT

What are you doing to Joe?

ELLEN

Why don't you mind your own business?

(She turns around, swinging her wand at Grant. As she sees Grant and he sees her, the wand hits him gently in slow motion in the chest. We hear a crash in the background. The spotlight forms a halo around Ellen and Grant. She holds the wand in an erect position. Ellen and Grant are staring at each other. The manager tries to pull Ellen away. The audience is booing the manager.)

ELLEN

Mary, Mary!

(Mary comes running over, the burly drunk right behind her. Mary pulls at the manager. The drunk pulls at Mary. To help her, Ellen grabs Grant's jacket and tears his tuxedo label.)

MANAGER

(Looking back at Mary in costume . . .) Another one!

(The Burly Man is wearing Mary's hat.)

ELLEN (pointing to Grant) Mary, look!

MARY

(Takes Ellen's wand and hits Grant with it . . .)   What did you do to my friend?

ELLEN

Mary, look. Green eyes.

(She points to Grant.)

Green eyes!

(The Manager pulls at Ellen again.) Wait a minute, what are you doing?

(Ellen pulls away from him.) Who are you?

MANAGER

I'm Peter Pan. Come on, let's go!

(The audience is booing the manager again, they're having a great time.)

ELLEN

(To the manager, pointing at Grant) Who's that?

MANAGER

That's Grant Michaels, the singer.

MARY

Ellen, let's get out of here.

ELLEN

Mary look, he has green eyes. Mary, grayish brown hair.

GRANT

(Touching his hair . . .) Brown.

THE AUDIENCE

(In unison . . .)

28

Grey!

MARY

Ellen, I see what'you mean. Green eyes, brown hair,
the psychic was right.

(pause)

Ellen, you've found him, you found my soul mate.

Ellen takes the manager's flower and puts it into
Grant's lapel.

ELLEN

Mary, he's wearing a flower - (she tells the audience)
– he's wearing a flower.

(Grant doesn't know what's happening. He takes the
flower out of his lapel. He holds it in his hand. Mary
is also confused.)

ELLEN

Green eyes . . . (She looks at Grant) . . . brown hair . . .

(Ellen puts the flower back into Grant's torn lapel.)

And Mary, he's wearing a flower. The psychic was right. She was right! We found my soul mate!

MARY

You already have one.

ELLEN

I lied.

A GIRL

(The girl Grant was singing the love song to whispers to the manager . . .)

Who did she say he was?

MANAGER

Her mate or something, I don't know. I didn't even know he was married.

GIRL

(Getting up to leave . . .)

I knew he had someone else in his life!!!

30

ELLEN

Mary, the psychic was right.

(To the Burly Man . . .) The psychic was right.

BURLY MAN

I'll drink to that!

HIS DATE

You'll drink to anything.

(He picks up a drink from one of the tables.)

CUSTOMER

Hey, that's my drink!

ELLEN

(Imitating Katharine Hepburn . . .) Drinks for everyone!

(teasing the manager)

Mr. Pan, I would like to buy everyone a drink.

GRANT

Who did she say she was?

MANAGER

Your soh mate.

Three women near the manager get up and leave, throwing their napkins at Grant.

MARY

(to Ellen)

Ellen, what are you doing? Drinks for everyone? Are you crazy?

ELLEN

I saw Katharine Hepburn do that in a movie once. I think it was Katharine Hepburn.

(Ellen does her imitation of Katharine Hepburn.)

ELLEN

Drinks for everyone!

She looks over at Grant, he's trying to straighten himself out.

ELLEN

Grant Michaels, Grant Michaels.

32

The waiters are cleaning up.

MANAGER

(To the audience . . .)

The lady would like to buy everyone a drink.

The audience applauds. The manager turns to Mary and Ellen.

MANAGER

Would you ladies like a table?

MARY

No, we're leaving.

ELLEN

(In her best Katharine Hepburn voice . . .)

A table, yes, I think we would love a table.

(She looks at Grant, who is standing, his jacket is torn, napkins are hanging from his shoulder, his hair is messed up. Ellen tries to patch his jacket with a pin from her hat. She fixes the flower and dusts him off with a napkin.)

ELLEN

You really don't sing like a rooster.

GRANT

Thank you.

ELLEN

It's more like a donkey in heat.

GRANT

Now that's funny!

ELLEN

Thank you. But I have a question.

GRANT

What!

ELLEN

Do I really walk like King Kong?

GRANT

No, but keep practicing.

34

(He laughs. Ellen hits him in the stomach with her
wand. Then she touches him with the wand on his
shoulder. She presents Grant to the audience . . .)
Voila!

(The audience applauds. The spotlight is turned on.)

ELLEN AND GRANT (Standing together . . .)

Hi!

GRANT (Gestures toward Ellen, Grant is staring at
Ellen and smiling.)

Let's give the star of our show a hand.

(They give her a standing ovation, she takes a bow.
Mary pulls her out of the spotlight as the manager
finds a table for them. Grant turns to the pianist. He
starts to sing. Looking in Ellen's direction, he blows
her a kiss; Mary is getting jealous.)

MARY

Let's go to the Ladies Room.

ELLEN

Grant is singing. Where's my drink?

MARY

That's a funny name for a song. Come on, let's go.

ELLEN

I don't want to leave. Not now.

MARY

Just to the Ladies Room. Come on.

(Mary grabs Ellen's arm. They go to the Ladies Room. Ellen is walking backwards, looking back at Grant.)

INT. LADIES ROOM, HOTEL - NIGHT

ELLEN

Mary, he has green eyes. He's fantastic!

MARY

Let's get out of here.

(She looks up at the window.)

ELLEN

Mary, do you think he likes me?

36

MARY

We should have gone straight home. Ellen, you're in trouble! What happened to that superwoman who had complete control of her emotions? Soul mates are for dreams, remember, they're not meant to be real. Ellen, you're a married woman. Psychics tell everyone the same thing. It's a female fantasy. Ellen, wake up!

ELLEN

Yes, but did you see how cute he was?

MARY

No one can be that pretty and be single. What will your mother say?

ELLEN

I wonder if he's married?

MARY

I think she would assume he was. Come On, let's get out of here before it's too late.

ELLEN

Mary, it's early. One drink.

MARY

I thought you didn't drink.

ELLEN

He's driven me to it.

MARY

Oh, boy!

(Mary pushes the chair to the window. She stands on it, measuring the width of the window. She comes down and measures Ellen's rear end.)

MARY

You're lucky.

(She measures herself.)

I may have to borrow your girdle.

ELLEN

I never knew I could talk like Katharine Hepburn. You know, I liked being in the spotlight. I think the audience liked me. Mary, do you think the audience liked me?

38

MARY

You're making a fool of yourself. Quick, out the window!

(Mary cups her hands to boost Ellen up to the window.)

ELLEN

(Looking in the mirror . . .)

Oh Grant, Grant.

(Imitating Katharine Hepburn again . . .)

Wherefore art thou, Grant?

MARY

Ellen, think of your wonderful family. Your beautiful home. The good life.

(Ellen starts singing "Loving Him.")

MARY

Uh oh. You're pretty far gone.

(Ellen then hums loudly over Mary's words, blocking them out.)

ELLEN

But Mary, you don't understand. He's so cute.

MARY

I never realized how vulnerable you are. Come on, it's still not too late.

(The window leads to the hotel garage.)

MARY

Ellen you can't handle this kind of emotion. You're not ready. I'm the one who's ready! If it had happened to me . . .

ELLEN

If <u>what</u> had happened to you?

MARY

(Wailing . . .)

Nothing! Nothing happens to me.

ELLEN

One drink and then we'll go.

Ellen splashes water on her face and puts on a

40

little makeup.

ELLEN

Do you think I made a good impression on him?

MARY

I would say he's impressed. You tore his jacket,
disrupted his act, ruined his chances with that blonde
he was singing to . . .

ELLEN

She's old enough to be his mother!

(They leave the Ladies Room.)

INT. CABARET ROOM - NIGHT

(They enter again and walk to their table. Grant is
standing at the bar.)

ELLEN

There he is, at the bar. He doesn't even remember
me.

(They watch the attractive blonde walk over to Grant
and talk with him.)

ELLEN

I'll kill her. Why is he talking to her?

MARY

Did you hear what you just said?

ELLEN

What?

MARY

Kill, you want to kill her. You've turned into a killer. You, the preacher of universal love. The spirit of goodwill. You've become corrupted and perverted –

ELLEN

(Not paying any attention to Mary.) Why is he letting her stand so close to him?

MARY

Maybe he's cold?

ELLEN

(Calling the waiter over . . .)

42

Please tell Mr. Grant Michaels that if he doesn't' come
over to our table right now I'll do the scene from
"Frankie and Johnnie."

(The waiter approaches Grant and whispers in his ear.
Grant looks over at Ellen and smiles, then he gives
the attractive blonde a kiss on the cheek and walks
over to Ellen's table. He pulls the chair out to sit and
moves her pocket book.)

GRANT

Hi!

ELLEN

What did you do that for?

GRANT

Do what?

ELLEN

Do what? Do what?

(She turns to Mary . . .)

Tell Mr. Short-Memory what he just did!

MARY

He pulled out the chair, then sat down and said hello.

GRANT

I said hi?

(She and Grant look at each other and shrug, like what's up with her?)

ELLEN

You kissed that girl! You kissed her right in front of me. How could you do that to me?

GRANT (getting defensive)

She's my cousin?

ELLEN

Your cousin! Why are you lying to me? How can I ever trust you?

GRANT

(Grant calls the manager over) Tell her who that young lady was who I was talking to.

44

ELLEN

<u>Kissing!</u>

THE MANAGER

(As if he's said it a hundred times)

His cousin.

(The manager turns and walks away.)

ELLEN

Your cousin! You really expect me to believe that?

(Grant and Mary look at each other, confused. Ellen pinches Grant's cheek.)

ELLEN

Relax, I'm only teasing!

(She's laughing, they all start to laugh. Grant has the same reaction he had when she did her imitation of Katharine Hepburn. She has a strange quality and he's getting caught on the hook. She's already caught.)

ELLEN

Promise me one thing.

GRANT

What?

ELLEN

Promise me you'll never kiss her again.

(They look at each other with a twinkle of love in
their eyes and they laugh.)

MARY

There goes the good life!

ELLEN

(to Grant)

Well, what do you think?

GRANT

I think you're crazy. Who the hell are you?

ELLEN

Oh, I almost forgot. We don't know each other,

do we? Grant, this is Mary Kohler. And I'm Ellen Taylor.

GRANT

Hi Mary Kohler. Hi Ellen Taylor.

(He kisses Ellen's hand, she feigns a swoon.)

ELLEN

I love it, I love it!

(She looks at her hand, at the kiss, she notices her watch)

It's eleven o'clock. It's late, Mary. It's eleven o'clock already!

MARY

It was late an hour ago. Now it's just eleven o'clock.

ELLEN

Grant, we have to go.

GRANT

It's early. Where are you going?

MARY

I know where I'm going. I don't think she knows where she's going.

(Grant has a confused look on his face.)

GRANT

(As they get up to leave – to Ellen)

When will I see you again?

ELLEN

How about tomorrow? Where do you live?

Grant hands her his card.

GRANT

Nice meeting you, Mary.

MARY

You don't have a twin brother, do you?

Grant kisses Ellen on the cheek.

ELLEN

I thought you only kissed your cousins on the cheek.

GRANT

48

(He kisses her on the lips.) See you tomorrow.

(Mary pulls Ellen away. The audience applauds as they leave. Ellen takes a bow.)

ELLEN

(Imitating Katharine Hepburn.) Thank you, thank you, thank you!

MARY

Come on, Ellen.

(Mary looks back and sees the attractive female walk over to Grant. Ellen starts to turn around. Mary pulls her before she gets a chance to see Grant talking with the attractive female.)

FEMALE

(to Grant)

Well, you should be able to add another notch.

GRANT

She's not that kind of female. She's my soul

mate.

(They both start to laugh.)

MANAGER

Hey, she forgot to pay the check!

GRANT

I'll take care of it.

(Grant looks at the check.) $1,700.00!

MANAGER

(with a bad Katharine Hepburn imitation) Drinks for everyone!

EXT. HOTEL PARKING AREA — NIGHT

Ellen and Mary walk through the parking area.

MARY

Ellen, tear his card up. Forget about him. You know what's going to happen if you see him again. He's a gigolo.

ELLEN

But Mary -

50

MARY

You're not going to see him tomorrow, are you?

ELLEN

Mary, what should I do?

ELLEN

You're asking me? That's not fair.

You're happy with your life.

ELLEN

I do have a good, comfortable, happy life, don't I?

(Mary shrugs her shoulders.)

At least I thought I did. But tonight was different.
Strange. Mary, for the first time in my life I feel
excited. I have feelings in my body I never knew
existed. He kissed my hand. I never knew what that
meant. I can't explain it, maybe I should go and see
that psychic again. What do you think?

MARY

I think you should see a shrink instead.

Seriously, we should <u>both</u> forget about him. Come on, let's go home.

ELLEN

He is kind of cute though, isn't he?

Mary kisses Ellen on the cheek.

MARY

Tomorrow this will all seem like a bad dream. Ellen, tear his card up and let's go home.

(Ellen pulls something out of her bag and tears it up.)

MARY

Why don't we have lunch tomorrow?

ELLEN

That's a good idea.

Mary kisses Ellen on the cheek

MARY

Let's go back to the real world.

(Ellen turns around to go back to the club. Mary

52

pulls her away, they're both laughing.)

MARY

Come on, Cinderella, we're outta here!

INT. LIVING ROOM, GRANT'S APARTMENT - DAY

The living room is large and nicely furnished. Grant is talking to the doorman via an intercom downstairs. He is dressed casually in tan slacks and a pullover sweater.

GRANT

Okay, send her up.

(Grant paces around the room a little nervously. All of a sudden there is a knock at the door. He opens it. It's Ellen. She's garishly dressed in a multi-colored dress and wearing too much makeup. She takes one look at his face.)

ELLEN

You're not happy to see me. It's too early. Someone else is here. One of your cousins slept over. What? What is it?

GRANT

Where do you get your costumes?

ELLEN

What costumes? I thought you would like me dressed this way. Like the girls in the club. I look that bad?

GRANT

(laughs and walks her over to a mirror)

See for yourself.

ELLEN

(she looks, she grimaces) I'm going home, I look terrible.

GRANT

Wait here. No, maybe you'd better sit down.

(He sits her down, away from the mirror and disappears into his bedroom, then comes back out with a pair of jeans and a pullover.)

GRANT

Here, go into the bathroom and change.

54

ELLEN

(Taking the clothing, he walks her over to the bathroom door, she pauses before going in.)

Did you miss me?

GRANT

Of course I did. I mean, we haven't seen each other for what?

(he looks at his watch) -- almost twelve hours.

ELLEN

Has it been that long?

(Ellen puts her elbow into his stomach and winks, then kisses him on the cheek. She goes into the bathroom as he goes to the stereo and puts on some music. She comes out of the bathroom, and it's the first time we've really gotten a look at her. She looks fantastic. Her hair is pulled back, the jeans are a little loose but she looks great. He has a startled look on his face. She looks like the sunshine of his life.)

ELLEN

Now what? You still don't like the way I look? (she looks down at her jeans then looks in the mirror) Not enough makeup. It was a mistake to come here. Mary was right.

GRANT

Come here. You look fantastic!

(Grant holds her in his arms, she's getting a little nervous. She tries to divert his attention.)

ELLEN

This is a nice apartment.

(she starts walking around) Good color-coordination.

GRANT

Not as good as yours.

ELLEN

Did you do the decorating yourself?

GRANT

No, I had a decorator.

ELLEN

What's his name?

56

GRANT

What's who's name?

ELLEN

Your decorator.

GRANT

Oh. Karen Jones.

ELLEN

Oh, Karen Jones. Is she young?

GRANT

80 or 90. I can't remember.

ELLEN

Pretty?

GRANT

No.

Pretty?

ELLEN

She's pretty, isn't she? Why can't you be honest. Tell the truth, you like her, don't you?

GRANT

I haven't seen her in over a year.

ELLEN

Any children?

GRANT

What children?

ELLEN

You and your decorator?

GRANT

Sure, I gave her three children instead of paying her.

ELLEN

She works cheap.

(The phone rings. He goes to answer it. She starts rearranging some of the furniture.)

58

GRANT

(into phone)

Hi! How are the children? I'll try to stop by next week.
Good. Take care,

(Grant hangs up the phone.)

ELLEN

Who were you talking to?

GRANT

(teasing her) Oh, just my decorator.

ELLEN

I'm out of here.

(She gathers her things and heads for the door.)

GRANT

Where are you going?

ELLEN

You're not my soul mate, you're a gigolo.

GRANT

Now wait a minute -

(The phone rings again, he goes to answer it. Ellen goes to the door, making a half-hearted attempt to open it. He hears the lock turn. Grant hangs up the phone and runs to stop her from leaving.)

(He trips into her. They pause and look at each other. Grant takes her hand, they hug each other tight. He goes to lock the door and sees that the lock was never opened. He takes her bundle of clothing and tosses it on one of the chairs. She looks very sad.)

GRANT

What's the matter?

ELLEN

Who was that on the phone?

GRANT

It was a wrong number.

ELLEN

Wrong number.

60

(She gets up to leave again. As she pulls away, he holds her back with one hand and reaches for his neck, faking pain, trying to distract her.)

ELLEN

Wrong number? 'How are the children?'

GRANT

Oh! That call? That was my brother. He has three children.

ELLEN

So do I.

GRANT

So do you <u>what?</u>

ELLEN

Have three children.

GRANT

Three children?

(He reaches for his neck. Now it is hurting.)

ELLEN

Lie down.

GRANT

You didn't. tell me.

ELLEN

Sssshhh.

(Ellen starts to work on his neck. He pulls her down
to him and kisses her. She's startled and swoons.)

GRANT

What's the matter?

ELLEN

I don't know. I think I'm going to be sick. Do you have
something to drink?

GRANT

How about some coffee?

ELLEN

Coffee!

62

GRANT

What's wrong with coffee?

ELLEN

Don't you have any herbal tea? Some ginseng or
soybean mix? Carrot juice?

GRANT

(looking at her a little confused)

Who are you?

ELLEN

I'm your soul mate, remember? The girl you've been
singing about? Now that we've found each other
again, we're going to be together for all eternity this
time.

GRANT

What do you mean this time? Eternity?

ELLEN

I went to my psychic this morning before coming
here. She said we were together in our past lives. But
they wouldn't let us be happy.

GRANT

(Condescending, he kisses her on the cheek) Who wouldn't let us be happy?

ELLEN

The Gods, of course. You see, you were a king, and you ruled in a cold, rugged country. Your subjects were barbarians. I was a princess born into a very highly developed culture. That's why they wouldn't let us be together. You weren't ready for me then. But now you are.

(she's smiling)

So here we are! Promise me, you won't see that decorator again? Or drink coffee?

(she looks at her watch) Oh, it's almost twelve!

GRANT

What happens at 12? Do we go back to our past lives?

ELLEN

No, I have to call my husband.

She starts dialing the phone.

64

GRANT

Your husband!

ELLEN

Ssshhh.

(Ellen puts her finger to her lips then starts talking to her husband.) What time are you leaving?

(Just then the apartment door opens and in walks a very attractive young lady, Grant's roommate.)

SANDY

Hi!

(Sandy walks toward the kitchen and pulls out some coffee from a shopping bag.)

I picked up some more coffee.

(Sandy goes into the kitchen. Ellen stares after her.)

ELLEN

(hanging up the phone) What was that?

GRANT

A can of coffee?

ELLEN

Who was that?

GRANT

Sandy, I want you to meet Mrs. Taylor.

Sandy stops in her tracks, turns around, smiles.

SANDY

Hi Mrs. Taylor. Don't mind me.

(Sandy goes into her room and hears Ellen say-)

ELLEN

I'm leaving!

(she tears at Grant's pullover) Who is that?

GRANT

She's my cousin's friend's daughter. She's from Texas.
She wants to be an actress. They asked me to help her
until she gets on her feet.

66

ELLEN

She'll never be on her feet living here. Where are my things?

GRANT

Come on, she's just a kid. She has her own room. We hardly see each other. She's only been here a couple of weeks.

SANDY

(calling out from her room)

Grant, is Mrs. What's her name still here?

GRANT

(smiles at Ellen and yells back) Yes!

SANDY

Then I better put some clothes on.

She comes out scantily clad.

SANDY

(to Ellen)

Don't mind me. Are you an actress too?

GRANT

No, she -

ELLEN

(interrupting him)

Yes, I'm an actress and a writer. In fact, I'm writing a play about a barbarian king who is murdered in his apartment.

SANDY

Really? That's great!

GRANT

(looks at Ellen, he is smiling) She's a housewife.

SANDY

Wow! That must be very rewarding.

GRANT

She has three children.

SANDY

Wow! Really?! Three children!

68

Sandy goes back into her room.

ELLEN

(imitating Sandy) Wow, really!?

GRANT

She's a nice kid, isn't she? And a good actress. She needs a break.

ELLEN

A break, you creep.

(she tears at his sweater again) Do you really want to help her? I mean, with her acting career?

GRANT

Of course I do.

ELLEN

Of course you do. I know someone in the theatre. Maybe he could find something for her to do.

(imitating Katharine Hepburn)

In the theatre.

GRANT

I'll tell her to send him a picture and resume. What's his -

ELLEN

Let me call him right now.

GRANT

(Grant goes to the bookcase and pulls out Sandy's picture.)

Here. She has her own phone. The number's on her resume.

ELLEN

(looks at the picture and dials)

Hello Bruce?

(Ellen talks to him for a minute or two, low and friendly, we can't hear her. Grant, in the meantime, goes to the bar to make them both a drink.)

Thank you Bruce. I knew I could count on you. I love you too.

(She hangs up the phone.)

70

GRANT

Who is Bruce?

ELLEN

Oh, he's just a relative on my mother's side.

GRANT

(offering her the drink)

How about some lunch? Hey, you didn't tell me you had a mother.

(He kisses her on the cheek, she backs away.)

GRANT

What's the matter now?

(Sandy comes running out of her room screaming.)

SANDY

I'm going to be – a star! I'm going to be a star! I just got a call for a job. They're opening a new theatre in Alaska. I leave in a week. Isn't that great?

(to Ellen)

I'm sorry we won't have more time to get acquainted. I probably could have learned a lot from you. About acting. Writing. And life - and -

(Sandy goes to Grant and kisses him.) This has been the best year of my life.

(She walks back towards her room.)

ELLEN

(kicks Grant in the shins) A few weeks?

GRANT

Come on, she's exaggerating! She's an actress!

SANDY

(turns around to Grant)

Grant, we'll have a whole week to celebrate.

ELLEN

(quickly)

Grant, can I use your phone again?

GRANT

Sure. I think I have a bottle of champagne. Let's

72

celebrate.

(Ellen makes her call as Grant is looking for the champagne.)

GRANT

(a little jealous) Who are you calling?

ELLEN

Bruce.

GRANT

Tell him he missed out on a future star.

ELLEN

Yes, I think he'll say he's going to kill himself.

(into phone)

Hello, Bruce?

She whispers into the phone again, and then hangs up, smiling.

GRANT

(smiling)

Sandy, come out here and celebrate.

Sandy reappears and they pour champagne and toast to her future.

GRANT

To Sandy, a star in every way.

(In the background we hear a phone ringing. Sandy goes to her room, singing.)

SANDY

(singing)

A star is born, a star is born!

GRANT

(to Ellen)

You brought her luck.

(He goes to kiss her. Sandy comes running out of her room.)

SANDY

They really need me. Wow. I have to leave tonight. I start rehearsing tomorrow morning. I better start packing. I think I have some of my things in your bedroom. Isn't life exciting?

ELLEN

(imitating Sandy) Isn't life exciting?

(They both laugh. He grabs her, she pushes him away
and gives him a dubious look.)

ELLEN

'Things in your bedroom?!'

(He pulls her to him and kisses her. She returns his
kiss with passion.)

SANDY

(coming out of her room) Isn't he great?

Ellen pinches him, he drops his champagne glass.

SANDY

Oh, I'll clean it up.

(to Ellen)

You're probably cleaning your house all the time.

(Sandy bends over, she is scantily clad. She exposes her rear end to Grant.)

ELLEN

(under her breath) I'll kill her.

SANDY

Cleaning is fun, isn't it?

She exits singing "A Star is Born."

ELLEN

I hate you.

GRANT

You hate me? A mother with three children and a husband. What kind of a soul mate are you anyway?

ELLEN

That all happened before we met.

GRANT

Oh, that's different. I should have realized. After all, we've only known each other –

76

(he looks at his watch)

Let's see...you couldn't possibly have had three
children in 14 hours, could you?

ELLEN

How many children have you had? And don't forget
little Sandy.

GRANT

None.

ELLEN

How many wives have you had?

GRANT

20 at last count.

ELLEN

Very funny. If you play your cards right you may
make Black Jack.

GRANT

If I play my cards right; I should have stopped playing
last night.

ELLEN

You did. How do you like me so far?

GRANT

I don't like you so far. (Grant brings her to him.)
Come closer,

Ellen allows a long kiss, he starts walking her to his
bedroom. She stops.

ELLEN

I want to talk to you about something.

GRANT

Why do women always want to talk? What do you
want, to sell me insurance?

ELLEN

That's right, insurance. Aside from all of your cousins,
who else knows about you? Why isn't a talented
performer like you successful? What you need is a
new direction, ah, a new act.

GRANT

What are you talking about? What do you know

78

about being an entertainer?

ELLEN

It all came to me last night after I left you. I never
told anyone this before but I've always dreamed about
entertaining, acting and singing.

GRANT

What does all that have to do with my needing a new
act?

ELLEN

We're going to work together.

GRANT

What am I not getting here?

ELLEN

The act. I'm going to be in your act.

GRANT

You're kidding!

ELLEN

I'm not. With our talent and my connections, we'll
have our own TV show in no time.

GRANT

I work alone.

ELLEN

Now you're starting to sound like Garbo.

Grant laughs.

ELLEN

Why don't you want to work with me? I'm not pretty
enough? You want someone like that female at the
club? You don't love me, you're not my soul mate.

GRANT

<u>Who</u> doesn't love you?

(He picks her up to carry her to his bedroom, holding
her in his arms he kisses her.)

80

ELLEN

Put me down you beast. You scoundrel! You cad, you -

(She launches into her Katharine Hepburn imitation again.)

GRANT

What film is that from?

ELLEN

How should I know? How was I?

GRANT

Lousy. You don't want to be an entertainer.

(He sets her down.)

ELLEN

Come on, I really do have connections.

GRANT

Have you ever performed?

ELLEN

Are you kidding? You saw me last night. Do you think keeping three kids entertained is not performing? I'll take lessons. Well, what do you think? When do we start?

GRANT

(not really serious) Tomorrow. Hi partner.

(Grant shakes her hand.)

ELLEN

The first thing we have to do is get you out of this apartment. Too many distractions. I want you to move in with me and the children.

GRANT

(he's laughing) You and the children?

ELLEN

What's so funny?

GRANT

Did you say move in with you and the children? I don't like children.

82

ELLEN

Don't let Sandy hear you! Who said you have to like
them? Anyway, when they learn about you, they
won't like you either. And besides, it's a big house.

GRANT

Let me get this straight. You and I have known each
other not even one full day and you want me to give
up my apartment and move in with you and the
children? Am I right so far?

(Ellen nods her head.)

GRANT

Now you have no experience as an entertainer,
correct?

(Ellen gestures as if "well, I wouldn't go that far.")

But you had a dream last night and now you want to
be an entertainer. Excuse me, not just an entertainer,
but you want to work with me, as a team.

(She nods, in a cute way, yes.)

GRANT

It's all clear to me now. You're not looking for a soul mate. What you want is a cell mate.

ELLEN

Grant, trust me. I know it all seems strange. But we were together in our past lives. And we're going to be together again now. We can't stop destiny.

GRANT

Ellen, you want me to move in with you and your children. What about your husband?

ELLEN

Oh, I forgot about him. What am I going to do about him?

(a long pause)

He seemed more important yesterday.

(She has a tear in her eye. Grant hugs her.)

GRANT

Come on, superstar. Let's have something to eat.

84

(Sandy comes out of her room singing -)

SANDY

A star is born, a star is born! I'll be right back.

(Ellen and Grant look at each other and laugh.)

GRANT

What do you feel like eating?

ELLEN

Are you going to cook for us?

GRANT

Sure, unless you want to.

ELLEN

Want to what?

GRANT

(kisses her on the cheek) Cook!

ELLEN

I can't.

GRANT

Thought you said you were a mother.

ELLEN

I am but Tet Sut -

GRANT

God bless you!

ELLEN

Thank you. But God Bless Tet Sut. He does all the cooking.

GRANT

What's a Tet Sut?

ELLEN

He's our chauffeur's son.

GRANT

Your chauffeur's son is your cook? Who cooks

86

for the chauffeur?

ELLEN

Tet Sut's mother.

GRANT

(laughing)

Why doesn't Tet Sut's mother cook for you and your family?

ELLEN

Because she runs the house. Anyway, Tet Sut is afraid of water.

GRANT

Tet Sut does the cooking. Because he's afraid of water?

ELLEN

The kitchen doesn't have a swimming pool.

GRANT

I thought all kitchens had swimming pools.

ELLEN

The swimming pool is in the living room. Anyway,
Tet Sut loves to cook. He gets to chop food and Kung
Foo at the same time.

GRANT

Your cook is a black belt Kung Fooer?

ELLEN

No, he has a brown belt. I have a black belt.

She goes into a Kung Foo stance.

ELLEN

Do you want to Kung Foo around?

GRANT

The only belt I own is a Gucci. What the hell are you
talking about?

ELLEN

You see how well we work together? What else do you
want to know, nosey?

88

GRANT

Nothing.

ELLEN

I have three children. Two boys, Andrew and Steven. The seventeen-year-old Andrew is 6'2" and weighs in at 220 pounds as of yesterday. Steven, the fifteen-year-old, is not big but gaining quickly. Then there's Susan. She's 11 and the only thing growing on her right now is her impatience.

GRANT

What about all that Tet Sut Kung Foo swimming pool business?

ELLEN

All true. We do have a swimming pool and a father and a mother to go with our Tet Sut. My husband makes a lot of money and our investments, knock on wood -

(she taps his shoulder)

are doing very well. What about you?

GRANT

What do you feel like eating?

ELLEN

What about you?

(she pinches his cheek).

You weren't born in this apartment.

GRANT

No, I was born into a tribe of barbarians, remember?

(reaching out to grab her)

We ate raw meat.

He kisses her, she's swooning.

ELLEN

Why don't we call a Chinese restaurant?

GRANT

I have a better idea. Why don't we call Tet Sut and tell him to send over some chopped liver?

90

ELLEN

How old are you?

GRANT

How old are you?

ELLEN

I mean . . . 37.

(Ellen looks into her drink).

What the hell is this? Truth serum? I usually say 33.
How old are you?

GRANT

33.

ELLEN

Come on, how old are you? Be serious.

If we're going to be working together . . .

(she smiles)

We have to be honest with each other.

GRANT

Okay, I'm not really 33.

(trying to change the subject) How about some food?

ELLEN

How about rehearsing our act?

GRANT

I thought we were.

ELLEN

Wise guy!

GRANT

You're not serious about being an entertainer, are you?

ELLEN

Oh really. Watch me. As my great uncle used to say "You ain't seen nothing yet!"

GRANT

Al Jolson was your uncle?

92

ELLEN

Who's Al Jolson?

GRANT

Who's Al Jolson? He was only one of the greatest
entertainers who ever lived. Come on, you don't
know a thing about entertaining.

ELLEN

(singing)

Swanee, Swanee, How I love you. (then) How old are
you? How old are you?

GRANT

39.

ELLEN

That's the perfect age. How long have you been 39? I
mean, how long have you been singing?

GRANT

About 10 years.

ELLEN

What else have you done – that you can talk about?

GRANT

(smiling)

Not much. I worked in the family business for a while. Have you ever had a 'charlotte rouse' or a 'Melo-Roll?'

ELLEN

I love Melo Rolls. We had Melo Rolls in Philadelphia.

GRANT

The Siciliano Sunshine Ice Cream Company, Brooklyn, New York.

ELLEN

Siciliano, that's Italian.

94

GRANT

That's a-right. What were you doing in Philadelphia?

ELLEN

Well, if you were ever in Philadelphia and had a prescription filled or bought some-

(she pauses)

you were probably in one of my father's drugstores. BEST Pharmacies. Hey, I can make an egg cream for us.

GRANT

Let's call a Chinese restaurant.

(Sandy reenters the room carrying a gift for Grant.)

GRANT

What's this for?

SANDY

For being so kind to me.

(She looks at Ellen and Grant.)

It looks like you finally found that special person you've been looking for. For that boy and girl act you've been talking about.

(She kisses Ellen and Grant on the cheek and goes back into her room.)

ELLEN

What act?

GRANT

Come on, let's go to a drugstore and buy some ice cream.

ELLEN

Grant, I'd love to.

(She looks at her watch).

But it's getting late and I have to go. Tet Sut's mother and father are on vacation this week. I've got to be home before my daughter comes home from school. Why don't we have lunch tomorrow at my house?

(Ellen writes her phone number and address and directions on a piece of paper.)

96

ELLEN

Here, how about 12, or 12:30?

(They're kissing standing by the door. Just as she's leaving Sandy calls out -)

SANDY

Grant, can you give me a hand?

ELLEN

Maybe I could stay a little longer.

(Ellen looks at her watch)

No.

GRANT

(Kisses her again) I'll see you tomorrow.

(The phone rings) Call me when you get home.

(Ellen leaves. Grant closes the door.)

SANDY

Grant!

INT. HALLWAY, GRANT'S APARTMENT - DAY

ELLEN

(Hears this) Damn it!

(Ellen is standing by the closed door with her ear to the door. She finally leaves.)

INT. GRANT'S APARTMENT - DAY

(Sandy comes out of her room.)

SANDY

Grant, I want to thank you again for –

GRANT

Grant puts his finger up to his lips.

Sshh!!!

(He gives her a hug.)

Hey! Do you really have some of your things in my bedroom?

SANDY

No, I was just teasing her. You know, the way she looks at you. I think she's in love and I saw a little twinkle in your eyes as well.

GRANT

98

Okay, superstar, go twinkle and get packing.

(He sings "A Star is Born" "A Star is Born" to tease her.)

GRANT

What movie was that from?

SANDY

What?

GRANT

Nothing.

(Sandy goes to her room.)

INT. SANDY'S ROOM - DAY

(Sandy starts packing, throwing her things into a bag.
She looks in the mirror, puts on some lipstick,
brushes her hair and then launches in to "I Want It
All" as she continues to pack.

She finishes the song as she closes her bag. She exits
the room.)

INT. GRANT'S LIVING ROOM - DAY

(Sandy hugs Grant and he kisses her on the cheek.)

GRANT

Go and chase your dream. Nothing can hold you back.

SANDY

Not even three kids and -- ???

GRANT

Get going, superstar!

(She leaves. The phone rings and Grant picks it up.)

GRANT

Hello? Hey, Magen, how are you? When did You get back from Paris? Lunch tomorrow? Great, what time? 11:30 at the club?

Wait a minute, I can't. I'm driving out to Long Island tomorrow. No, just business. Call me next week . . . look forward to seeing you, too.

(Grant goes to the window of his

apartment. which reveals a southern view from the 34th floor of his apartment on East 79th Street. It's night and all of Manhattan is alight. He has a JFK-in-the-Oval-Office "Cuban Missile Crisis" look on his face.)

INT. ELLEN'S HOUSE - DAY

(Ellen is on the phone with Bruce. She is over-dressed, looking very "Hollywood." It's almost 12 noon.)

ELLEN

Bruce, hi, Ellen. Bruce, I have this fantastic entertainer coming over to the house today. I want to do something with him. I want to put together a whole new act for him. Bruce, he's fantastic. I need your help. Get me the best person in the business to work with. I want the top man. That's right, to put an act together. Send him over at, let's see. 3 o'clock. Bruce, I'm serious. Hire a limo. I know you can do it. By the way, you were great with Sandy. Sandy the superstar! I want you to meet him. Come over at...we'll need about two hours. Make it 5 o'clock. Oh, and Bruce, call Robert. Find out what it will cost to videotape an hour's TV show. I want to package and syndicate the show. I already spoke with my neighbor Sy. If he likes the idea he'll sponsor us. He made millions on that business connection we made for him last year.

Oh, and call Cousin Seymour. Tell him his record company can have the first shot at our first album. And Bruce, I want you to manage us. Bruce, I'm going to be in the act. I'll explain it all when I see you. Don't forget, 5 o'clock. What's whose name? Oh, Grant Michaels, Grant Michaels. Love you.

(She hangs up and looks at her watch. She's fidgeting. Lunch is being prepared by Tet Sut. The phone rings again.)

ELLEN

Mary, how are you? I was talking to Bruce. He's fine. Wait, slow down. Who was made president? Your husband? Mary that's great. He's taking you to Europe? For a month? Fantastic. Take your ballet shoes. Mary, leave your girdle at home. And remember, if you want to be seen completely naked, you have to leave the lights on. Who? Grant?

Grant who?

(pause)

Oh <u>that</u> singer! Mary, you have to be kidding. Why would I go to his apartment? Are you crazy? And do what? Mary, bite your tongue.

Yes, he was cute. No, I tore his card up. I don't have the pieces. I burned them. Mary, you're going to Europe next week for a month. I'm not sure if we can make it tomorrow night. He's out of town. Let me call you tomorrow. And Mary, get rid of that mirror. Love you.

(Ellen hangs up. Her son and daughter come into the room.)

ELLEN

Kids, we're having company for lunch. A new friend. Someone I'm going to be working with.

STEVEN

(her youngest son)

Why are you wearing sunglasses?

SUSAN

(her daughter)

She looks just like a movie star. Mom, you look just like a movie star.

STEVEN

She does look kind of strange, doesn't she?

SUSAN

(to Steven)

You're going to look strange.

(Susan starts chasing him into another part of the house; Ellen's talking to Tet Sut).

ELLEN

Tet Sut, our guest is a very special person.

TET SUT

When is Mr. Taylor coming home?

ELLEN

Sometime tomorrow.

(The kids come running out. Steven is chasing Susan; she runs into Ellen's arms. Tet Sut takes a Kung Foo stance as Steven comes at Ellen and Susan. Tet Sut stands between them. Steven stops dead in his tracks.)

ELLEN

Now, kids, this is an important meeting. So I expect you both to behave. And Steven, no Kung Fooing with our guest. Remember what

104

happened to Uncle Moise?

STEVEN

That was his fault. If he didn't weigh 300 pounds he wouldn't have broken his arm when he fell. All I did was -

(He demonstrates his Kung Foo stance; Ellen goes into a moderate Kung Foo stance as well.)

ELLEN

Look, I'm serious. I want you to behave.

STEVEN

Who is this guest? Why do we have to be so serious? Why are you all dressed up in the morning? When is Dad coming home?

ELLEN

Tomorrow.

SUSAN

Mom, who's coming over?

ELLEN

Someone I recently met. He's a singer. I met

him with Mary.

SUSAN

Is he on TV? Is he famous?

ELLEN

Right now only his cousins know how good he is. But he's going to be famous when he gets his own TV show.

SUSAN

Mom, are you going to help him get on TV?

ELLEN

I hope you're going to like him. Where's your brother?

STEVEN

He went to pick up his car at the body and fender shop.

SUSAN

Mom, what time is he coming?

106

ELLEN

He should be here any minute now. He's coming in by train.

(she looks at her watch)

I told him to call from the station.

STEVEN

Doesn't he have a car?

SUSAN

Doesn't he have any money?

ELLEN

I told you, he is a successful entertainer.

STEVEN

Does he make as much money as Dad?

ELLEN

How should I know?

SUSAN

Is he married?

ELLEN

No. He lives with a girl named Sandy. No, he's not
married. He lives alone.

STEVEN

Hey mom, you know a guy who lives with a girl and
they're not married? What would grandma say?

ELLEN

She's say mind your own business! Just be nice to
him, okay? I want him to feel at home.

(We hear a car horn, and the kids run to the window
as Tet Sut answers the door. Ellen is nervous. She
looks in the mirror, fixing her hair, then sits in a chair
with her back to the door, trying to act nonchalant.
She picks up a book, she thinks Grant has arrived.
She doesn't realize that it's not Grant but Mary. Mary
walks over to Ellen, she taps Ellen on the back.

ELLEN

That's a pretty light tap for a soul mate.

MARY

I didn't think you cared.

108

ELLEN

(turning around, startled) Mary, what are you doing
here? I told you I burned the card.

MARY

Where are the ashes?

(laughs)

I forgot to tell you on the phone we have to return
the costumes. We should have returned them
yesterday but it seems you weren't home when I
called. Tet Sut said Mrs. Taylor left very early. How
<u>was</u> the green-eyed monster?

ELLEN

Mary, what are you talking about? I told you I didn't
go to his apartment. I went shopping. I was home by
1:30. What time did you call?

MARY

9:30, 11, 12:30, 2 o'clock.

ELLEN

You must have dialed the wrong number.

MARY

Ellen, come on. Unlike you, I wasn't born yesterday. I know you went to see him. You don't have to tell me everything, just tell me what happened.

ELLEN

Mary, I'm surprised at you. You know I wouldn't go to a strange man's apartment. In all the years we've known each other, have I ever once been with another man?

MARY

As a matter of fact -- No.

ELLEN

So what makes you think I would start now?

(Mary is moving her mouth.)

ELLEN

Mary, what are you doing?

MARY

I'm biting my tongue. Come on, let's bring the costumes back and have lunch. I'm supposed to

110

meet Rose at 2 o'clock. She's dying to hear about our affair.

(Mary is laughing.)

ELLEN

Mary, don't you dare tell her about what's his name?

MARY

Grant? What is there to tell? We had a drink and got involved in a barroom brawl. You beat up the club manager. Chased away a few customers. And met some singer with green eyes and brown hair. What is there to tell?

ELLEN

Don't forget, he was wearing a flower. Let me get the costume.

(Ellen leaves.)

MARY

(goes over to Tet Sut)

Who is Mrs. Taylor expecting?

TET SUT

I think Mr. Taylor is supposed to come home today.

MARY

Thought he was coming home tomorrow?

ELLEN

(comes back with the costume) Come on, let's go. We'll take your car.

(she pauses, snaps her fingers)

Oh, I forgot! The plumber is coming to fix Susan's bathroom.

MARY

What's wrong with her bathroom?

ELLEN

The return valve regulator is broken. Mary, do you mind returning my costume? I have to stay here and give the plumber a check. You know they won't work unless they know they're going to get paid.

112

MARY

What time is he coming?

ELLEN

He was supposed to be here by now.

MARY

I'll wait. It's early.

(The phone rings and Ellen answers it. It's Grant and he's lost.)

ELLEN

Hello? Oh hello dear. Where are you? At the airport?

(Ellen holds her hand over the phone, talks to Mary)

It's my husband.

(Ellen talks into the phone again)

A what? Taxi strike? No, they're on vacation, remember? I'll come to the airport to pick you up. Relax, at the main terminal. Got it. And relax, have a drink. I'm leaving right now.

(Ellen hangs up)

Mary, I have to go to the airport. There is a taxi strike.

MARY

I'll wait for the plumber.

ELLEN

Mary, the heck with the plumber!

MARY

I'll go with you. We can return the costumes
tomorrow.

ELLEN

Mary, stop it. I'll have enough trouble at the airport.
Come on, let me change.

(She tries to walk Mary to the door. We hear a horn.
Susan runs to the window. Steven comes running out
when he hears the horn.)

STEVEN

Wow, look at that!

114

SUSAN

Wow, look at that! Wait until Daddy sees–

STEVEN

Is he going to be jealous! Wow, look at that car!

(They run to the door.)

ELLEN

Sugar! Tet Sut, answer the door.

(Tet Sut just barely beats the kids to the door. He goes into his Kung Foo stance. The kids stop and let Tet Sut open the door. Grant is standing there, looking like a super attractive well dressed movie star. The kids have startled looks on their faces. Mary sees it's Grant, she looks at Ellen.)

MARY

Rats!

(Mary goes to the door to leave.)

GRANT

(To Mary as she's walking out.) Hi Mary!

MARY

Are you sure you don't have a twin? Talk to you later, Ellen.

(Mary leaves.)

GRANT

Tet Sut.

TET SUT

God Bless You.

GRANT

I didn't sneeze.

TET SUT

We say God Bless you to everyone who enters this house for the first time.

ELLEN

Kids, this is Mr. Grant Michaels. Grant, this is Susan, Steven and Tet Sut.

(Right behind Grant is Andrew, the oldest son, he's a huge kid.)

116

ANDREW

Whose car is that?

ELLEN

Andrew, this is Mr. Michaels.

ANDREW

(To Grant) How fast can it go?

GRANT

(Looking at his weight) 220 pounds.

ANDREW

Can I try it?

(Grant looks at Ellen; she doesn't say anything.)

GRANT

Sure.

(Grant flips Andrew the keys.) Just don't change its shape.

ANDREW

Are you kidding? I'm a fantastic driver. I've had

my license for, tell him, mom. Over six months now.

(He exits. A minute later we hear the sound of
screeching rubber.)

ELLEN

Well, what do you think?

GRANT

I think it will never be the same.

ELLEN

Your life?

GRANT

My car.

(Grant reaches out as they are walking to put his arm
around Ellen. Steven doesn't see this but Susan does.
She gently kicks him in the shins and walks between
Ellen and Grant.)

ELLEN

Kids, I want you to find something to do. Mr.
Michaels and I have a lot of business to discuss.

SUSAN

What time is Daddy coming home?

ELLEN

Soon.

(She kisses Susan and pats her on her rear end and the kids leave the room. Susan looks back at Grant and gives him a dirty look.)

ELLEN

I think they like you. Did you bring your music?

GRANT

What was all that about the airport, taxi strike, have-a-drink-honey business about?

ELLEN

I thought you were coming out by train?

GRANT

I changed my mind.

ELLEN

You were only three blocks away, I told you to

wait, I was going to come and pick you up as soon as
Mary left.

GRANT

Where was I supposed to wait? The main terminal?

ELLEN

Did you bring your music?

GRANT

What music?

ELLEN

To rehearse the act.

GRANT

Ellen, do you know what it takes to put an act
together? We'll have plenty of time to rehearse. First
we'll have to have some special material written for
us, I have a friend in California, he'll be back in New
York in about two weeks.

ELLEN

In two weeks we'll have our own TV show.

120

GRANT

Why do we have to wait so long?

(He turns around to leave, teasing her.)

GRANT

I'm leaving.

ELLEN

Okay, one week)

GRANT

That's different.

(He looks around the house; it's fantastic.)

GRANT

It's a pity you have to live in this tenement slum.

ELLEN

Yeah, pretty shabby, huh? But we call it home. I know you're used to living in the Playboy Mansion. With your little bunny rabbits.

GRANT

You mean my ex-bunny rabbit? Sandy left this morning.

ELLEN

Did she get a good night's sleep? Or should I say, did she let <u>you</u> get a good night's sleep?

GRANT

She kept me up all night – (smiling) – talking.

ELLEN

She talks in her sex. . . I mean in her sleep?

GRANT

She was very excited. She's waited for a break like this for a long time. You know, she really liked you.

ELLEN

Really?

GRANT

It seems she was never close to her mother.

122

He laughs.

ELLEN

Only close to her father.

(She kicks him in the shins.)

GRANT

Where's your husband?

ELLEN

What do you want to do, sell him insurance? I
thought you came to see me?

GRANT

I came for one of Tet Sut's famous Kung Foo meals.

(They walk to the table.)

GRANT

Where's the chopped liver?

(They sit at the dining room table. Ellen rings a tiny
bell. Tet Sut comes out with a fantastic platter of
multi-colored vegetables. Grant looks at them.)

GRANT

That looks like one of your dresses.

ELLEN

I resemble that remark.

(They both laugh.)

ELLEN

You have me mixed up with your decorator. Tet Sut, serve the Miso soup please. He's going to need all the protein and energy he can get. He's going to have a very busy afternoon.

GRANT

What are we going to do?

ELLEN

We're going to make all our dreams come true.

GRANT

When do we start?

ELLEN

(she looks at her watch) Soon.

124

GRANT

Tet Sut, bring me some more soup.

(then, when he does)

What's that floating to the top?

ELLEN

That's Miso, soy beans.

GRANT

Don't you have any chicken soup?

ELLEN

Why, do you need some penicillin?

GRANT

Haven't you heard of preventative medicine?

ELLEN

That's very clever, why don't we put it in the act?

GRANT

I thought it was.

(She throws a piece of celery at him. From outside we hear car tires screeching, then Andrew reenters the room.)

ANDREW

What a car! I beat Dr. Bengus' custom phantom. He looked like he was standing still. I would have been home sooner but I was stopped by your friend, what's that cop's name? The one you and Tet Sut gave those herbs to? To grow hair? I had to let him take the car for a spin. He said to tell you the stuff you gave him is really working.

(Andrew tosses Grant the keys.)

What a car!

(He exits.)

ELLEN

How long have you had the car?

GRANT

I bought it to drive up here.

Ellen looks at him, shocked.

126

GRANT

I'm kidding. A little over a month. If I'm lucky it may last another week. By that time you'll be a star.

ELLEN

Very funny. I think your idea is great.

GRANT

What idea? I don't have any ideas. I'm innocent. Ask Tet Sut if you don't believe me. Tet Sut, do I have any ideas? Where did he go?

ELLEN

The idea that Sandy said you had, about finding someone to work with? The act?

GRANT

Oh, <u>that</u> idea! You have quite a memory. I thought by now you had forgotten about the act. I mean, you haven't mentioned it for almost 30 seconds. Why are we wasting so much time? Let's start rehearsing right now. Let's find a quiet room and -

ELLEN

Let's wait for our coach.

GRANT

You mean our couch?

ELLEN

Bruce is sending someone over to work with us. Oh, I forgot to tell you, if we're lucky maybe Bruce will manage us.

GRANT

Bruce? What makes you think I want someone by the name of Bruce to manage me? What makes you think I need a coach? What makes you think I want to work with you or anyone else? I told you, I work alone. Look, I like you. You're attractive, intelligent...

ELLEN (teasing)

What else?

GRANT

You have a nice family. A nice house.

128

ELLEN

A good family, a good house.

GRANT

A good life. So do I. Why can't we just be good friends?

ELLEN

Why don't you take some of this good food and wear it?

(She throws a handful of gooey food at him and he throws some at her. They're both a mess, covered with food, sitting at the table, laughing. Tet Sut comes out to see what's happening. They both throw food at Tet Sut. They're all laughing. The phone rings. Tet Sut answers the phone, it's for her.

ELLEN

Tet Sut, show Mr. Michaels where he can wash. Bruce, hi!

(she's still laughing)

We just finished our lunch. You checked on who? Grant? You're kidding. What did you find out?

He was a captain in the Air Force? Wrote three spy novels? One was on the bestseller list for what? Nine months? You're kidding! He turned down two Hollywood contracts. Bruce, is he married? I'm here. I heard. Never married. Bruce, maybe he doesn't want to be a star. Maybe he's happy with his life. Why am I pushing him? Why don't I leave well enough alone? Why don't I drop the project? Bruce, you're kidding. I want to be star. He's fantastic. Bruce, you're fantastic. Did you make all the arrangements? Good, see you at five. Love you, Bruce.

(Grant comes back.)

ELLEN

How do you like Tet Sut's cooking?

(Grant takes a little piece of food off her face. She does a turn.)

ELLEN

Doesn't his food taste and - (she does another turn) -- look great?

GRANT

Who was that on the phone?

130

ELLEN

Someone you'll meet later.

(Ellen walks Grant over to the bar.) Tet Sut, make Mr. Michaels a drink. Let me go and change.

TET SUT

What would you like to drink?

GRANT

A little Drambuey on the rocks. Tet Sut, where is Mr. Taylor?

TET SUT

Mr. Taylor is away on business.

GRANT

When will he be back?

TET SUT

Tomorrow. Morning.

GRANT

Does he go away often?

TET SUT:

Mr. Taylor is very busy man. He travels a lot.

GRANT

You like Mr. Taylor?

TET SUT

Mr. Taylor very nice man.

GRANT

Is he young?

TET SUT

Mr. Taylor much older than Mrs. Taylor. You going to work with Mrs. Taylor?

GRANT

I don't know. Maybe.

TET SUT

She needs to get out of the house more. Good for her and the children.

132

GRANT

Tet Sut, you like Mrs. Taylor?

TET SUT

Mrs. Taylor special lady.

GRANT

You're a special person Tet Sut.

TET SUT

Thank you Mr. Grant.

ELLEN

(returning) Who's a special person?

(Tet Sut leaves.)

GRANT

(Grant kisses her hand) <u>You're</u> a special person.

ELLEN

Grant, there's something important I want to tell you.

GRANT

You changed your mind? You don't want to be in the act?

ELLEN

Would you be happy if that was true?

GRANT

Not really.

ELLEN

Do you like me?

GRANT

You know I do. I liked you from the moment you – . . . tried to upstage me.

(They both laugh, then –)

ELLEN

Really? Do you think we could work together?

GRANT

As my old Uncle Al used to say, you haven't tried until you've tried.

134

ELLEN

Your Uncle was in show business?

GRANT

No, he's a lawyer.

(They both start laughing. They're in love.)

ELLEN

Speaking about uncles, wait until you meet my Uncle Robert. He's the shortest in the family. He wanted to be a doctor like his brothers but he couldn't stand the sight of blood so he went into television. Now we call him a TV surgeon. All he does is cut this program, cut that program. Cut, cut, cut. Well, it's his television station. If we're lucky, maybe he'll perform a transplant. Cut one program out and put ours in.

GRANT

Ours? What program?

ELLEN

That's what I wanted to tell you. We're going to produce our own TV show.

(The doorbell rings. Ellen goes to the door. Grant is sitting down, we hear Ellen talking to "the coach." As she approaches Grant to introduce him to Grant, Grant turns around.)

GRANT

Max, what are _you_ doing here?

(to Ellen)

This is our coach? Max Herm. He's the best in the business. I thought you were in Europe.

MAX

I was. I got back two weeks ago. Bruce Besig asked me to do him a favor.

GRANT

Bruce Besig? You don't mean Bruce Besig the head of NGA?

MAX

That's the only Bruce Besig I know.

Grant looks at Ellen and smiles. She tilts her head.

136

MAX

So you two want to put an act together? Let me take a look at you.

(Max puts them together.)

Not bad.

(Ellen takes off her sunglasses and makes a modified Kung Foo stance.)

Not bad at all. How long have you two been together?

(Grant looks at his watch.)

MAX

You know, with a little bit of luck you two could become very big. I'm not kidding. Bruce told me to discourage you but I think you two have something special. I'd like to work with you.

(Ellen shakes Max's hand.)

ELLEN

We're ready.

MAX

(looks at his schedule book) How about starting our first session, let's see . . . next Tuesday?

ELLEN

Max, we could rebuild Rome by next Tuesday. What time is it?

GRANT

3:30, General.

ELLEN

Thank you, Captain. We have an hour and a half before Bruce comes. Why don't we start now? Tet Sut, bring Mr. Herm a drink. What else do you need, Max?

MAX

Why not? Get me a pencil and some paper and make the drink. Carrot juice.

ELLEN

Max, you're fantastic!

(She kisses Max on the cheek and looks at Grant.)

138

ELLEN

We're on our way!

(Imitating Sandy)

A star is born, a star is born!

MAX

(Taking charge)

Now let's see, you're both attractive, intelligent. Ellen, you're a little more hyper than Grant so why don't we make you the catalyst?

(Asking Ellen)

Is that okay with you?

ELLEN

(Nudging Grant in the ribs.) I love it. I love it.

GRANT

Hey, he said catalyst, not pugilist.

(Max starts to write, Susan enters, goes over to Ellen.)

SUSAN

Mom?

ELLEN

Not now sweetheart. Go over to Joane's house until dinner.

SUSAN

Mom, help me with my homework?

ELLEN

Come on honey, mommy's busy.

(Grant pats Susan on the head, she tries to kick him in the shins. He skips. She misses. She walks away, sneering at Grant, and goes into her bedroom, as we hear Max say . . .)

MAX

Okay, I know _just_ where we need to start.

INT. SUSAN'S BEDROOM

(Susan sits down at her desk, her math books and homework spread out around her. But she can't seem to concentrate. She looks up at a photo of herself and her mother, and tears fill

140

her eyes. She begins to sing: "Mommy, You're Mine."
When she finishes we -

CUT TO:

INT. ELLEN'S LIVING ROOM - DAY

MAX

(Holding up a piece of paper –)

So we have a beginning, middle, and end. What do
you think?

ELLEN

This is what I've always wanted to do. I love it, love it!

MAX

It's fun, isn't it? But it can also and will be hard work
if you don't take it seriously. The audience will break
your heart if you let them down.

ELLEN

How can we let them down Max? We're great.

GRANT

We're <u>going</u> to be great, all right! But it's going to take more than just talking. We have a lot of work ahead of us. An act is not just two or three minutes of dialogue and a song. We're going to have to rehearse at least five days a week for a couple of months, right Max?

ELLEN

I love it. Max, a couple of months?

MAX

It depends.

ELLEN

Whatever the record is for putting an act together we'll break it. When I commit myself to something I'm in it all the way. Grant, we're going to have a lot of great things happening to us. Our timing is perfect. This could not have happened five years ago or 1000 years ago. And it won't happen five years from now. You'll see. All the pieces will fall into place. When something is right it has to happen. Nothing, or no one, can stop it.

142

GRANT

What film is that from?

ELLEN

I dunno, I read it somewhere.

GRANT

Where?

ELLEN

(She looks at the palm of her hand and his.)

Here.

(He grabs her hand and kisses it. The doorbell rings. It's Bruce. Ellen lets him in. They embrace at the door. Grant sees them, his face drops.)

BRUCE

(Sees Max)

Hello, Max.

ELLEN

(Ellen is holding Bruce's hand) Grant, I want

you to meet, my brother Bruce.

(Bruce shakes his hand, smiling.)

BRUCE

Hi Grant. You've certainly made an impression on Ellen.

GRANT

Like a fly in the eye of a tornado.

BRUCE

Well, Max, what do you think?

MAX

I think they work very well together. You would think they've been together for -

ELLEN

A thousand years, Max.

MAX

I was going to say 5,000 years.

144

ELLEN

Max, he wasn't here 5,000 years ago. He's not Jewish.

BRUCE

He's not?

MAX

Now you tell me!

BRUCE

Come on, . . . Max, let's go.

(They all start laughing.)

Max, are they ready for five hours of prime time?

MAX

How about a three-minute commercial?

ELLEN

We'll take the five hours!

BRUCE

Max, did you work something out for them?

MAX

We put together three or four minutes -

BRUCE

Okay, let's see what you two can do. Max goes to the piano, Ellen calls Tet Sut.

ELLEN

Tet Sut, dim the lights. And get the flashlight.

(Tet Sut dims the lights and .puts the flashlight on Ellen and Grant -)

MAX

And now, ladies and gentlemen, we proudly present Grant Michaels and Ellen Taylor -

(Ellen goes over to Max and whispers in his ear.)

MAX

For the first time this century, Ellen Taylor and Grant Michaels!

THE ACT

GRANT

Ellen, do you remember when we first met?

ELLEN

Of course I remember, Grant. It was the day we fell in love.

GRANT

You mean I <u>fell</u>. You poked me.

(She pokes him.)

I tripped and broke my fibula.

ELLEN

You broke your fibula? What's A fibula?

GRANT

It's a bone.

ELLEN

You didn't tell me you had a broken bone!

GRANT

Ellen, you were there by my side.

ELLEN

I'll always be by your side.

GRANT

And when my fibula became infected -

ELLEN

You did say 'leg bone?'

GRANT

Ellen, you were there by my side.

(She jumps into his arms and kisses him on the cheek.)

GRANT

And when the doctor said he had to cut my leg off – -
Ellen, you were there by my side.

ELLEN

I'll always be by your side.

148

GRANT

Ellen?

ELLEN

Yes Grant? Grant?

GRANT

Ellen, as I'm about to die – you're here by my side.

ELLEN

Grant, I'll always be by your side . . . For ever and ever. . . .

GRANT

(He drops her.

Ellen, Ellen – ?!

ELLEN

Yes, what? What?

GRANT

Ellen, you're – (pause) – a loveable jinx!

(Grant hands Ellen some music and together they
sing: "When A Love Like Ours Begins." After they have
finished singing the lyrics, Max continues to play the
chords while Ellen and Grant do some soft-shoe to
the end of the song. As the song ends it is clear that
Bruce loves the entire act.)

BRUCE

That was great!

(Bruce is clapping)

Bravo! Bravo! Max you were right, they are good.

ELLEN

Good? We're fantastic! We've had offers already. A
Hollywood producer, and CGI Management keeps
calling.

BRUCE

I'll match their offers.

150

ELLEN

You mean you'll give us a million dollars in advance?

BRUCE

(Bruce is laughing.)

No, I mean I'll match, burn their offers.

ELLEN

Hey Max, maybe we could work Bruce into the act. It looks like one of my talents has rubbed off on him.

BRUCE

You mean some of your talent was <u>ripped </u>off? Grant, I like it. I like the way you two work together.

(Susan enters the room.)

SUSAN

Uncle Bruce -

(She's running toward Bruce, and Grant makes believe he's going to catch her in his arms. Susan runs into Bruce's arms. She's annoyed

with Grant. She gives him a dirty look. Grant is
laughing.)

SUSAN

What was all that noise?

ELLEN

That noise – was our act – (Ellen points to Grant) and
Grant singing.

SUSAN

You call that singing? Blahhh.

Grant starts singing "Just For Love" to Susan.

SUSAN

(Running into Ellen's arms.) Mommy, make him stop!

(He sings closer to her face. Susan turns away.)

SUSAN

Mommy –

152

ELLEN

Come on, he likes you.

SUSAN

Well, I don't like him.

GRANT

She loves me, she loves me.

(He looks at his watch.)

Susan, you're not going to like this but I'm afraid it's getting late. Ellen, I have to get back to the apartment and take a shower and be at the club by 8:30. I'd better go.

ELLEN

Do you have to leave so soon?

SUSAN

Mommy, let him go.

GRANT

Max, do you want a lift back to the city?

MAX

No thanks, Grant, I have the limo waiting. Bruce, I'll speak to you tomorrow.

BRUCE

Grant, can you come to my office tomorrow morning? At say,11 o'clock? Max, I'll call you as soon as we decide what direction we're going to go with our superstars.

(They shake hands, Ellen kisses Max on the cheek. She goes to kiss Grant. Susan is watching. Grant kisses Ellen on the cheek. Ellen tells Susan to say good-bye to Max and Grant.)

SUSAN

Goodbye Max.

(She kisses Max on the cheek. She sticks out her hand reluctantly to Grant. He grabs her and pulls Susan to him. He gives her a big hug and a kiss on the cheek. Susan likes it. She forgets herself for a moment and returns his hug and kiss. She quickly pulls back and sticks her tongue out at him. Ellen and Grant are laughing. Ellen hugs Grant.)

154

(Max and Grant leave. We hear tires screeching. Bruce and Ellen and Susan walk into the living area. Bruce has his arm around Ellen and is holding Susan's hand.)

ELLEN

(to Bruce)

How do you like Grant?

BRUCE

I think the question is, how do _you_ like Grant?

ELLEN

(To Susan –)

Sweetheart, go and see if Tet Sut needs some help.

(Susan makes a face.)

ELLEN

Go on, Uncle Bruce and I need to talk.

(Susan exits.)

ELLEN

What do you mean, how do I like him?

BRUCE

Well, you look like a little girl with her first boyfriend.
You know you're a married woman.

ELLEN

But I feel like a little girl. I can't explain it, but it's a
whole new experience for me. I remember how I
used to laugh at my girlfriends when they talked
about their boyfriends. How they couldn't wait to see
them, be with them, being jealous. Can you imagine
actually being jealous? I used to tell them how stupid
they were.

BRUCE

Isn't it kind of late for you to do what you should
have done when you were younger? It would have
been easier.

ELLEN

No one ever made me feel this way before. I want to
work with him. I want to be with him. I could have
gone through my whole life like a robot. Numb. Do
you know that yesterday was the first time I felt any
movement in my body

and all he did was look at me and touch my hand? Do you know how many times I gave advice to friends about their feelings? Telling them to behave themselves, stop acting like fools. I had no idea what they were experiencing. No idea at all.

BRUCE

I'm not sure I know what you're talking about so I'm not going to give you advice. I just hope you know what you're doing. I want you to be happy. I've helped a lot of people, I guess I can help my . . . I almost said my baby sister. I haven't thought of you that way in years.

(Ellen hugs him, Bruce finishes his drink.)

BRUCE

See you tomorrow at my office.

(He gets ready to leave.)

Don't forget, 11 o'clock.

(Bruce turns to go.)

Oh, and one other thing –

ELLEN

What's that?

BRUCE

Why didn't you tell me you were a superstar?

(Ellen beams at Bruce and gives him a big hug. He leaves as Susan reenters the room.)

SUSAN

Mommy, don't forget about our school outing Wednesday. You promised to go.

ELLEN

We'll see. Go and do your homework. Go on.

(She nudges Susan to leave. Susan leaves. Ellen looks into a mirror.)

ELLEN

It's your fault. Why didn't you tell me? You teased me in my dreams. Why didn't you wake me up? You must have known that love was not a fantasy. I could have gone through my entire life like a robot, a damn robot.

(She's angry.)

158

I'm in control now.

(To the mirror –)

You're looking at a future star.

(The phone rings, it's her husband).

Hello? Oh hi. Fine. What time are you coming home? I have an appointment tomorrow morning. With Bruce. Nothing important. I'll tell you tomorrow. Nothing. I said nothing. Nothing's wrong.

(She hangs the phone up and kicks the table.)

ELLEN

Damn it!

SUSAN (reappearing) What's the matter, mommy?

ELLEN

Nothing. Did you do your homework?

SUSAN

That singer isn't coming here anymore, is he?

ELLEN

Go and finish your homework.

SUSAN

I need help.

ELLEN

I'll be there in five minutes. Now go to your room right now.

(Susan leaves crying. The doorbell rings. It's Grant. Ellen hugs him tightly. He has a little dog behind him. He shows her the dog.)

GRANT

I found this little dog on the backseat of my car. You don't by any chance, know who this little funny looking creature belongs to do you?

(Ellen takes the dog from Grant and cuddles it.)

ELLEN

Daisy. I didn't even know my little baby was missing.

(She kisses the little dog.)

160

Did you miss your mommy? Ah, poor little Daisy.
What did he do to you? Your life will never be the
same again.

GRANT

Neither will my car be the same again. Little Daisy,
tell your Mommy what you did on the back seat of
my car?

ELLEN

Daisy, wouldn't we like to know what he does on the
backseat of his car?

(He kisses Daisy, then Ellen.)

ELLEN

Was Daisy really in your car?

GRANT

No, I wanted to come back and talk to you. Are you
sure you . . . we . . . know what you're doing? You
realize that your whole life is going to change?

(Ellen starts to cry.)

What's the matter?

ELLEN

I just never realized how unhappy I was. I never realized how important being in love is.

GRANT

What about your husband? I mean, you must have loved him to marry him.

ELLEN

He's my second husband. I left my first husband. I had two little boys so I remarried.

(She's still crying).

He's much older than I am. He gave me the security I thought I needed. I hated every minute of our marriage. I can't tell you how many times I threw up after he touched me. I hate him. I hate him.

(Crying.)

I can't help it, I know it's a lousy thing to say but it's true.

GRANT

I'm curious about one thing. You have money,

connections. You have the drive and the talent to make it on your own. To be independent. Why did you stay in a bad relationship?

ELLEN

I don't know.

GRANT

Maybe you weren't ready.

(Grant smiles.)

Maybe you were waiting for me to come into your life.

(Ellen kicks him in the shins.)

This time we're going to be together forever.

(Grant kisses her.)

Sleeping beauty.

ELLEN

The question is, will they let us?

GRANT

It's in the hands of the gods.

ELLEN

I wish it was that simple. I mean, will my husband, my children . . . the lawyers, my mother, my grandmother in heaven. If only you were Jewish. Grant, no matter what happens, promise me one thing?

GRANT

Anything.

ELLEN

Promise me that you'll never see that decorator again.

(He hugs her and kisses her. Just then the phone rings. Ellen picks it up and speaks into it.)

ELLEN

Mary? What accident? Where? Pennsylvania coming from Miami? Mary, my husband's flight left from Miami! He called and said he had to make an unexpected stop in Pittsburgh. Mary, Let me go. He took an earlier flight!

164

SUSAN

(Off-screen) Mommy, where are you?

(Grant leaves. Ellen sings 'A Moment In Time.')

EXT. ELLEN'S HOUSE - DAY

Grant gets into his Maserati to leave. All of a sudden a Red Rolls Royce pulls into the driveway and a great-looking man (Cary Grant, Rock Hudson, (Len Guardino in a cameo role?), gets out and walks over to Grant. Grant gets out of his car.

HANDSOME MAN

Grant, I want to thank you.

GRANT

Who are you?

ELLEN'S HUSBAND

I'm Ellen's husband.

GRANT

I thought you were killed in a plane crash.

ELLEN'S HUSBAND

Oh, that was Mary's little joke. Grant, thank you for taking Ellen off my hands. She drove me crazy with her lousy Katherine Hepburn imitations. Look at my legs, she must have kicked me in the shins a hundred times. Oh, and Grant, when Mary and I come back from Europe, I'll expect you and Ellen and the three kids, the dog, Tet Sut and his family to be out of the house. I understand you have a big apartment. Mary can't wait to swim in the pool. She's ready to move in.

(He calls out to Mary, she opens the door of the red Rolls Royce and comes over to Ellen's husband. (Maybe she is wearing a tutu). She looks at Grant.)

MARY

(To Grant)

Wanna buy a mirror? Oh, and take this.

(She hands Grant her girdle. As Mary and Ellen's husband walk away arm in arm they are laughing and singing, "Just for Love.")

(We see Grant with the girdle in his hands.)

166

GRANT

(Stellaaahh ---)

Ellen, Ellen, where are you?"

(As the Credits Roll:)

CUT TO:

INT. GRANT'S APARTMENT - NIGHT

Ellen, Tet Sut and Tet Sut's family, Grant, Sandy, (in a mink coat), Susan, Ellen's sons and the dog are all crammed into Grant's apartment. Grant walks over to the window. He has a certain expression on his face, you guessed it, it's the JFK 'Cuban Missile Crisis" look.

SUSAN

Mornin, Grant come here! Your TV show is about to start.

(We hear the theme song from "I Love Lucy" then –

"Here are the stars of our show, Ellen and Grant!")

(Grant is standing behind everyone, watching TV. He reaches down to the bottom of the frame and pulls a plug. The screen begins to deflate like a balloon. We hear the air going "ssssss" then see a blank screen.)

Did it all really happen?

"Sans teeth, sans eyes, sans everything, sans Kings Point."

--William Shakespeare, circa 1600.)